P9-BBS-810

THE USBORNE BOOK OF
BABY ANIMALS

Susan Mayes

Designed by Non Figg

Illustrated by Rachel Lockwood and David Wright

Consultant: Gill Standring

Contents

Additional illustrations by Miranda Gray, Sean Milne and Chris Shields

Puppies

Many baby animals are helpless when they are born. They need lots of care, to help them grow strong and healthy.

Puppies cannot see or hear at first. Their mother feeds them with her milk, cleans them and keeps them warm. As they get older, they learn to do more and more. They grow playful and full of mischief.

Many animals have more than one baby at a time. A group of puppies born together is called a litter.

This puppy's little wet nose sniffs lots of new smells.

This is a mother Golden Retriever with her six-week-old puppies.

Puppies first open their eyes when they are two weeks old. They start to hear sounds when they are three weeks old.

Puppies need more sleep than adult dogs.

Having puppies

The male is the puppies' father.

The female is the puppies' mother.

To make puppies, a male and female dog mate. The male has a special liquid full of tiny things called sperm. This goes into the female.

Puppies grow in the female for nine weeks.

Some sperm meet tiny eggs in the female. This makes puppies start to grow inside her. When this happens, we say the female is pregnant.

The only food puppies need at first is their mother's milk.

The puppies are born one at a time and the mother licks them clean. Each puppy finds a nipple and drinks its mother's milk. This is called suckling.

As soon as a puppy's teeth start to grow, it chews almost anything.

The puppies below are play-fighting. This is a game which lots of baby animals play. It helps them test how strong they are and learn new skills.

A puppy's head seems quite big for its body. Its floppy paws look big, too.

These puppies eat some solid food now. They will soon stop drinking their mother's milk altogether. This is called weaning.

3

Rabbits

Most wild rabbits live underground in groups called colonies. They dig a home called a warren. It has lots of tunnels with rooms called burrows.

A male rabbit is called a buck and a female is called a doe. The doe can have a litter of babies every four weeks. Her babies are called kittens.

The mother dug this burrow, called a stop, to have her babies in. She made a grassy nest inside and lined it with fur from her body.

These babies were blind, deaf and hairless at first. Now they have soft fur and they can see and hear.

The babies cuddle up in their warm nest. They will not go outside until they are about three weeks old.

The mother comes to feed the babies with her milk once a day.

When the babies are four weeks old, the mother will leave them and go away to have some more.

Left alone

By the time the mother leaves her babies, they only need grass and plants to eat.

Each baby has to clean its own fur. This is called grooming. It helps the baby stay healthy.

A baby must use its long ears to listen for enemies. Its twitching nose can smell danger.

Deer

There are different kinds of deer all over the world. Nearly all of them live in forests and woodlands. Most female deer have one baby every spring. A baby deer is called a fawn.

Here are some white-tailed deer. There are lots of them in North America.

This fawn is only a few days old. Its big ears can already hear tiny sounds.

Big eyes look all around for enemies.

Deer can smell very well. A quick sniff of the air tells the fawn if danger is near.

The fawn stays very still and quiet when its mother goes to feed.

A spotted coat helps the fawn to hide from enemies. The spots look like sunny patches on the ground. Patterns that help animals to hide like this are called camouflage.

Long legs help deer to run very fast. This fawn is not strong enough to escape from danger yet, though.

Fawns start to eat grass and leaves when they are a few weeks old, but they need their mothers' milk too.

The mother deer's coat is plain. Some kinds of adult deer have spotted coats, like their babies.

In a few months, the fawn will lose its spotted coat, hair by hair. New hairs will grow to make a thicker, adult coat.

A clean start

The mother licks her newborn baby clean. After that, the fawn has almost no body smell, so it is difficult for enemies to sniff it out.

7

Hedgehogs

Hedgehogs are small, prickly animals. The ones you can see here live in Europe. The mother builds a safe nest under a hedge or a bush before her babies are born. She has four or five babies every summer.

When the babies are about four weeks old, they go hunting with their mother. They must learn to find food for themselves.

Baby hedgehogs are born without prickles, but they soon grow strong, spiky coats.

Hedgehogs cannot see very well, so they hunt by sniffing and listening.

Baby hedgehogs stay with their mother until they are about six weeks old. Then they go to live on their own.

Hedgehogs sleep in the day and hunt at night.

A baby hedgehog must learn to curl up into a tight, prickly ball. This stops enemies from hurting it.

These babies need to eat lots of food in the summer. This makes them fat, ready for winter when they sleep all the time.

Hedgehogs do not have prickles on their tummies. They have fur.

This baby is eating a meal of worms. Hedgehogs also like slugs, snails, beetles, caterpillars and frogs.

Another prickly animal

This animal has prickles, but it does not belong to the hedgehog family. It is a spiny anteater, or echidna. Mother spiny anteaters do not have live babies like mother hedgehogs. They lay eggs instead.

9

Beavers

Beavers are water animals. They live in families called colonies. Each colony builds its own home called a lodge. You can see a lodge on the next page.

The mother and father beavers stay together all their lives. Every spring, the mother has two or three new babies. They are called kits.

Kits make lots of noises. They grunt and squeak. They even snore when they are asleep.

The kits stay in the lodge for the first two months of their lives. Then they swim out for the first time.

This kit is paddling with its webbed back feet and steering with its tail.

Young beavers cannot hold their breath underwater for very long. Adult beavers can stay underwater for about 15 minutes.

Beavers love to clean and nibble each other's fur. This mother is grooming one of her kits.

Beavers build their homes from branches, stones and mud. They know how to build when they are born, but they must do it a lot to get really good at it.

Big, sharp front teeth are good for cutting down trees.

Beavers eat the outside layer of the wood, called the bark.

If there is danger, the older beavers will slap the water with their flat tails. The noise will warn the rest of the family.

Building a home

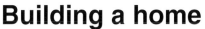

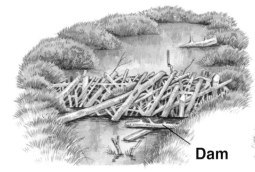
Dam

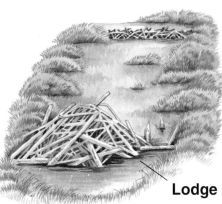
Lodge

First, the beaver family builds a wall across a stream, to trap water. The wall is called a dam.

The trapped water makes a pond. The family builds their lodge in it. They begin underwater.

The beavers are safe in their new lodge. They swim in and out through underwater tunnels.

11

Wolves

Wolves live in family groups called packs. In each pack there is one set of parents and their babies, called cubs. There are some other adults, too.

This is the cubs' father. He is the leader of the pack. He is the strongest, most important wolf and all the others obey him.

The cubs were born in a rocky den, in early spring. They are old enough to eat meat now, but they still need their mother's milk.

The mother is the strongest female in the pack.

Asking for food

The hungry cubs can hardly wait for a meal.

When an adult comes back from hunting, the cubs rush up to ask for food. They do this by licking its mouth. This makes the wolf bring up pieces of chewed meat for the cubs to eat.

The cubs have strong legs. When they grow up, they will be able to run for hours without getting tired.

Wolves learn to howl when they are very young. This is how they call each other to say, "Here I am". They also howl together before a hunt.

When the parents go hunting, other adults baby-sit and guard the cubs. They often help clean the cubs and bring them food, too.

Cubs start to learn about hunting by chasing and playing. Later, their parents teach them to catch small animals.

Each wolf in the pack has a special place in order of importance. They sometimes fight each other to prove who is strongest.

Wolf cubs learn to say things by using movements, sounds and smells. This cub is rolling on its back to say, "I give up".

13

Polar bears

Polar bears live in the Arctic Circle where it is cold and icy. In the winter, mother bears dig dens in the snow and have their babies inside. The babies are called cubs. They come out to explore in the spring.

First months

Inside the snow den, the new cubs snuggle up to their mother and drink her milk.

The cubs soon start to grow and play. Mother bear scratches snow away to make the den bigger.

In the spring, the mother digs a way out of the den. Her cubs follow her into the big, cold world.

Polar bears are the biggest kind of bear but they have the smallest cubs. The cubs in this picture were the size of guinea pigs when they were born.

The cubs soon learn to swim. They doggy-paddle with their front legs. They steer with their back legs.

This cub does not feel the cold. It has thick, oily fur and a layer of fat under its skin to keep it warm. These help it to float in the water, too.

Polar bears hunt seals. The cubs will learn to sniff the air to find food and track it down.

The cubs love to play. They chase each other, wrestle and slide around.

Polar bears have big, wide paws with fur on the soles, to keep out the cold. Their sharp claws grip the ice.

Cubs never see their father. Their mother feeds them, guards them and teaches them to hunt.

The snow and sun are very bright. Polar bears have a thin, invisible film over their eyes to keep the brightness out, like sunglasses.

15

Gorillas

Gorillas are big, shy and gentle. They live in family groups in the African rainforests. The parents take great care of their babies.

The silverback is the father of all the babies. He guards his family to keep it safe.

Silverback

Here is a family of gorillas. There is a big male leader called a silverback, some adult females and their young.

Most babies are born at night in nests made by their mothers. You can see a gorilla's nest below.

A young gorilla learns what to eat by tasting its mother's leftovers. Gorillas eat lots of wild plants.

Sharing a nest

Some nests are high in the trees. Others are nearer the ground.

Climbing is an important skill to learn. Gorillas climb trees to sleep and look for food.

Every night, each gorilla builds a nest to sleep in, using branches and leaves. A baby shares its mother's nest until it is old enough to build its own.

16

A new baby clings to its mother's tummy for the first few months of its life. Later, it rides on her back like this.

A female gorilla has one baby at a time. It grows inside her tummy for eight to nine months. This is almost the same time that a human baby takes to grow.

This mother will not have another baby until the one on her back is four or five years old.

Young gorillas learn to show good manners to the older gorillas in their family.

Gorillas are called knuckle-walkers because they lean on their knuckles like this. The baby in the picture will be able to walk by the time it is a year old.

Kangaroos

Kangaroos live in Australia. Their babies are called joeys. A joey spends the first few months of its life growing inside a pouch on its mother's tummy. Animals which grow in their mother's pouch like this are called marsupials.

Mothers and their joeys squeak to each other.

A joey drinks milk from nipples in its mother's pouch, but it soon starts to eat grass, too. The one in this picture is having a nibble without getting out.

A female kangaroo is called a doe.

A tiny baby

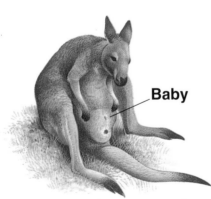

Baby

A newborn kangaroo is tiny, blind and helpless. It climbs up its mother's fur and into her pouch.

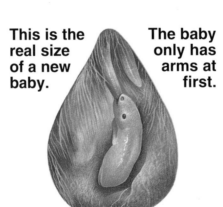

This is the real size of a new baby.

The baby only has arms at first.

In the pouch, the baby fastens onto a nipple and sucks milk. It stays there and grows slowly.

After a few months, the baby has all its body parts. It soon leaves the pouch for the first time.

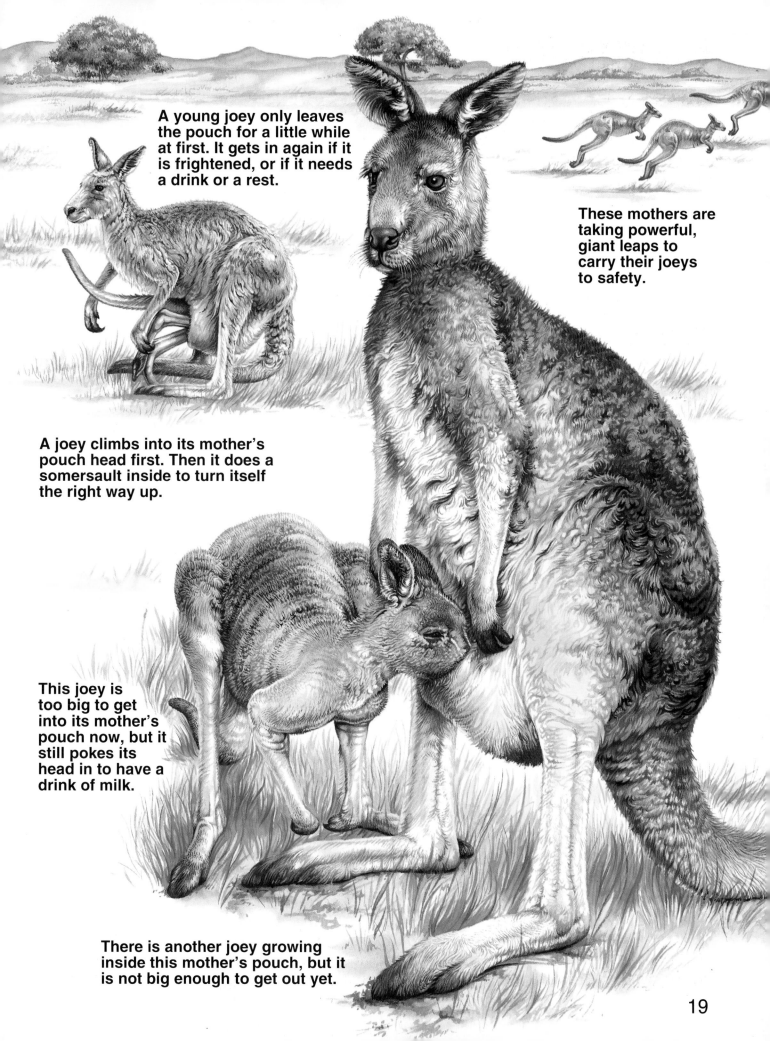

A young joey only leaves the pouch for a little while at first. It gets in again if it is frightened, or if it needs a drink or a rest.

These mothers are taking powerful, giant leaps to carry their joeys to safety.

A joey climbs into its mother's pouch head first. Then it does a somersault inside to turn itself the right way up.

This joey is too big to get into its mother's pouch now, but it still pokes its head in to have a drink of milk.

There is another joey growing inside this mother's pouch, but it is not big enough to get out yet.

Koalas

Koalas live in trees, in Australia. They look a bit like bears, but they are not bears at all. Koalas are marsupials, like kangaroos.

After a baby koala is born, it grows safely inside its mother's pouch for six months. Then it starts to ride around on her back instead.

At night, the baby climbs back into its mother's warm pouch. When it is nine months old it will be too big to get in.

A mother koala usually has one baby at a time.

This baby koala is clinging onto its mother's thick fur to stop itself from falling off.

The mother's pouch opens at the bottom, not at the top like a kangaroo's pouch.

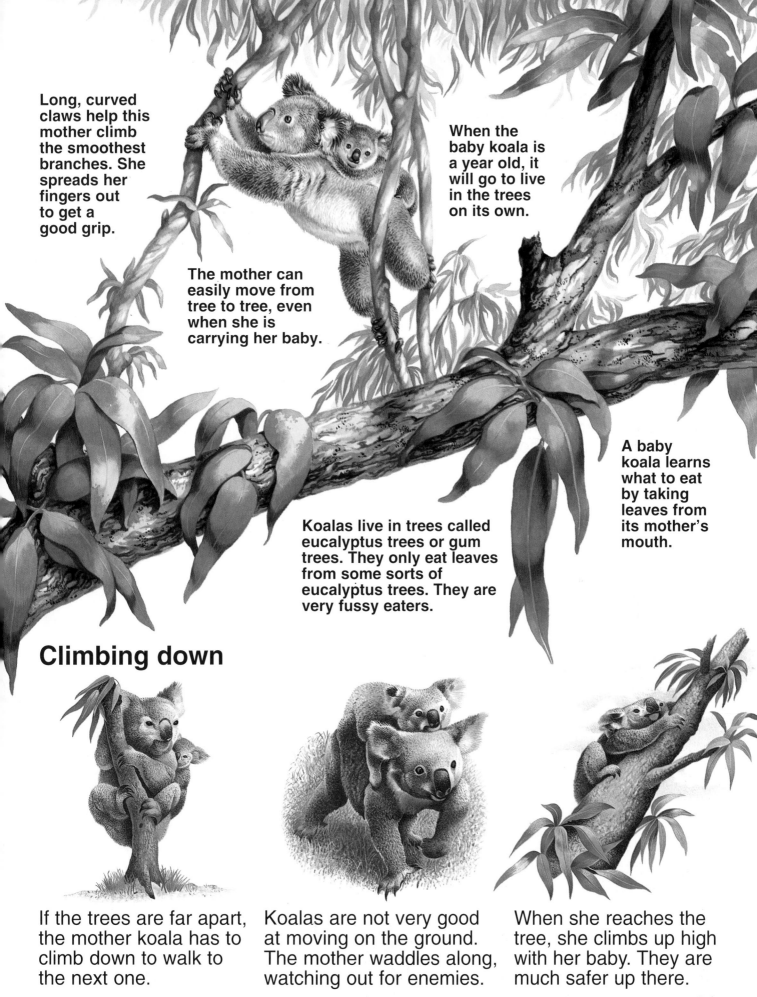

Long, curved claws help this mother climb the smoothest branches. She spreads her fingers out to get a good grip.

When the baby koala is a year old, it will go to live in the trees on its own.

The mother can easily move from tree to tree, even when she is carrying her baby.

A baby koala learns what to eat by taking leaves from its mother's mouth.

Koalas live in trees called eucalyptus trees or gum trees. They only eat leaves from some sorts of eucalyptus trees. They are very fussy eaters.

Climbing down

If the trees are far apart, the mother koala has to climb down to walk to the next one.

Koalas are not very good at moving on the ground. The mother waddles along, watching out for enemies.

When she reaches the tree, she climbs up high with her baby. They are much safer up there.

Elephants

Elephants live in groups called herds. Most of the elephants in the herd are females. The older males wander on their own or in small groups. Mothers take care of their babies with the help of the other grown-up females called aunties.

Being born

Mother

When a mother African elephant is ready to have her baby, the whole herd stops moving.

Auntie

The mother chooses one of the aunties to help her. The herd makes a circle to guard them.

The baby sucks milk with its mouth.

The new baby soon finds its way between its mother's legs to suck milk from her nipples.

Look at the baby standing between its mother's huge legs. It is about one metre (three feet) tall.

Mother elephants take care of their babies for longer than any other animal parent, except humans.

A baby elephant is called a calf. Its mother is called a cow.

Even new babies have thick, wrinkly skin like their parents.

The baby has big, flat feet to help carry its heavy body. Its feet look small next to the mother's enormous ones.

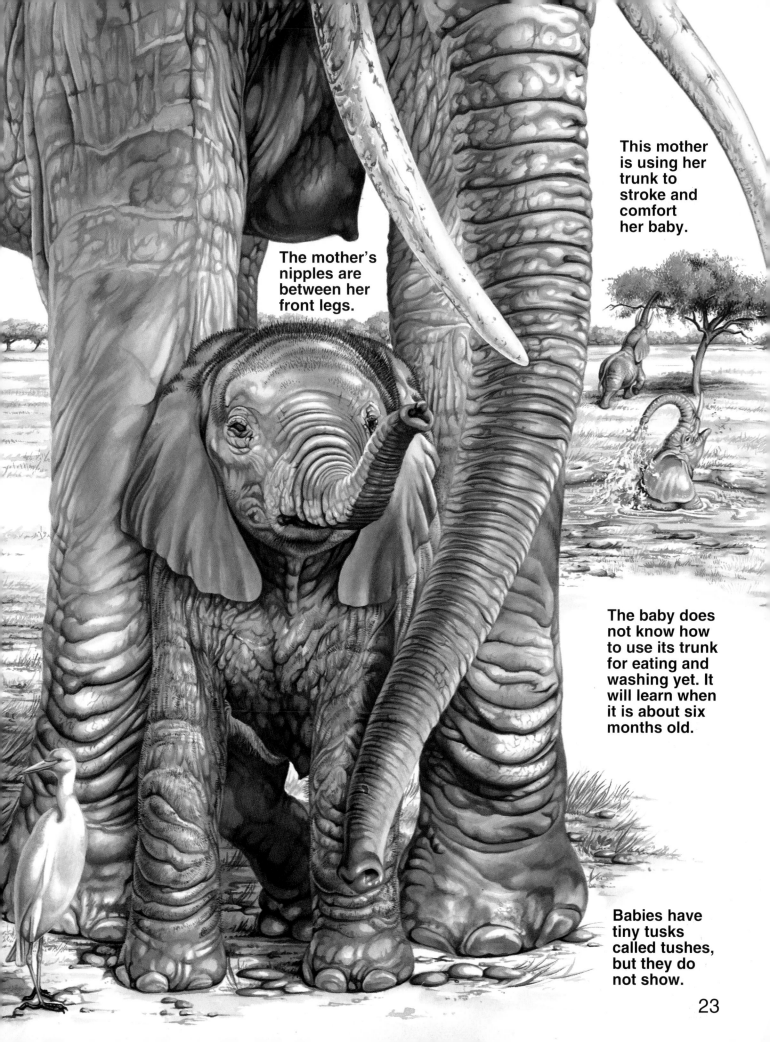

This mother is using her trunk to stroke and comfort her baby.

The mother's nipples are between her front legs.

The baby does not know how to use its trunk for eating and washing yet. It will learn when it is about six months old.

Babies have tiny tusks called tushes, but they do not show.

Zebras

Zebras are striped, wild horses. They live in Africa and roam around in family groups. Each group has one male called a stallion, five or six females called mares and babies called foals.

First steps

Birth sac

When a zebra foal is born, its mother licks it clean. It can already see, hear and smell.

Half an hour later, the foal can stand up. Its legs are very wobbly to start with.

The foal can run around after one hour. It has to run to follow its mother and escape from danger.

Every zebra has its own special pattern of stripes. Foals and their mothers know each other's patterns.

This foal is two weeks old. It stays close to its mother for safety.

These big ears are pricked up to listen for danger.

Foals have paler stripes than adult zebras.

These legs are long and spindly, but they are also very strong.

Zebras say, "Hello" to each other by sniffing noses. They sniff the air for danger, too.

The mother and foal know each other's voices. They grunt, snort and squeal. They even make a whistling noise.

Tigers

Tigers are the biggest wild cats. The babies are called cubs. Their mother is called a tigress. She usually looks after her cubs by herself. She guards them, feeds them and teaches them.

The cubs in this picture were helpless when they were born. Now they are very curious and they explore everything.

Cubs learn by playing and watching their mother. Pet kittens do this, too. You can see some on the next page.

The tigress brings her cubs meat from hunting trips now, but they still need her milk, too.

When the cubs are older, they will learn to hunt by copying their mother.

Moving home

A tigress often moves her new cubs to a safer place. She carries them gently in her mouth.

Tiger cubs "talk" with meows, coughs, squeaks and growls.

Cubs have blue eyes at first, but they soon turn yellow.

Cubs nuzzle and cuddle their mother to get her attention.

Kitten play

Pet kittens love to play, just like tiger cubs. The ones above are playing a stalking game. This helps them to learn important hunting skills.

Running and pouncing make a kitten strong and nimble. This would help it survive if it lived in the wild, like its big, striped relatives.

Seals

Here is a baby seal with its mother. The baby is called a pup. It was born on the ice, near the Arctic Circle.

The pup is only a few days old. It is called a whitecoat because of its soft, white fur.

The pup can hear the smallest sounds through its tiny ear-holes. It does not have ear-flaps like some animals.

This fluffy coat is not waterproof. The pup will grow a new, waterproof one when it is three or four weeks old.

The pup drinks lots of its mother's milk. It soon grows a thick layer of fat, called blubber, under its skin. This helps to keep it warm.

The front flippers have sharp claws. They grip the ice like hooks.

Seals have big eyes which help them to hunt fish in the dark water.

These seals have fierce enemies.
They are hunted by polar bears,
killer whales and Greenland sharks.

Grown-up male seals are
called bulls. They do not
have anything to do with the
pups. They stay in the sea.

The mother has one
pup every spring.
She sniffs it a lot, to
learn its smell.

A new coat

This pup is
called a
ragged
jacket
because
of its
scruffy
coat.

When a seal pup is
about three weeks old,
its fluffy fur starts to fall
out in tufts. Then its new
coat begins to show in
the gaps.

The pup's new coat is
silver with black spots.
It is not fluffy like the old
one. It is smooth and
waterproof. Seals grow
a new coat every year.

The mother will leave
her pup when it is
about two weeks
old. It will not
be able to swim
and catch fish until its
waterproof coat grows.

Whales

Here is a baby blue whale with its mother. The baby is the biggest baby animal in the world.

Blue whales spend most of the year in the icy seas around the North Pole and South Pole.

Born in water

A mother blue whale travels to warmer waters to have her baby. It is born tail first.

Whales cannot breathe underwater so the mother has to push her baby up to the surface for air.

Then the baby finds its mother's nipples. It drinks her milk while she floats on her side.

A female whale is called a cow. Her baby is called a calf. She has one every three years.

The mother and her baby look almost exactly alike. The only thing that is different is their size.

The baby was about 7m (23ft) long when it was born. That is about as long as four people lying end to end.

Whales listen to each other underwater all the time. Their ears are tiny openings in the sides of their heads.

Baby whales start to play and roll in the water when they are about three weeks old. They even jump into the air like the one in this picture.

Whales breathe air through holes on their heads, called blowholes. These are like our nostrils.

This baby is growing fast because it drinks lots of its mother's rich milk. She squirts it out of her nipples and into its mouth.

The baby always stays close to its mother, even when it is playing.

Deep underwater, it is too dark for the mother and her baby to see each other. They "talk" by making squeaks, whistles and lots of other sounds. They touch flippers, too.

Index

First published in 1994 by Usborne Publishing Ltd, Usborne House, 83-85 Saffron Hill, London EC1N 8RT, England. Copyright © Usborne Publishing Ltd, 1994.
The name Usborne and the device ♥ are Trade Marks of Usborne Publishing Ltd.
First published in America March 1995

All rights reserved. No part of this publication may be reproduced, stored in a retrieval system, or transmitted in any form or by any means, electronic, mechanical, photocopying, recording or otherwise, without the prior permission of the publisher. Universal edition.
Printed in Portugal.